P9-DOD-699

now

antoinette portis

A NEAL PORTER BOOK
ROARING BROOK PRESS
NEW YORK

Copyright © 2017 Antoinette Portis
A Neal Porter Book
Published by Roaring Brook Press
Roaring Brook Press is a division of Holtzbrinck Publishing Holdings Limited Partnership
175 Fifth Avenue, New York, New York 10010
The artwork for this book was created using sumi ink, brush, and bamboo stick. Color was added digitally.
mackids.com

Library of Congress Cataloging-in-Publication Data

Names: Portis, Antoinette, author, illustrator.
Title: Now / Antoinette Portis.
Description: First edition. | New York : Roaring Brook Press, 2017. |
    Summary: "Follow a little girl as she takes you on a tour through all of
    her favorite things, from the holes she digs to the hugs she gives"—
    Provided by publisher. | "A Neal Porter Book"
Identifiers: LCCN 2016038252 | ISBN 9781626721371 (hardback)
Subjects: | BISAC: JUVENILE FICTION / Family / General (see also headings
    under Social Issues). | JUVENILE FICTION / Concepts / General.
Classification: LCC PZ7.P8362 No 2017 | DDC [E]—dc23
LC record available at https://lccn.loc.gov/2016038252

Our books may be purchased in bulk for promotional, educational, or business use. Please
contact your local bookseller or the Macmillan Corporate and Premium Sales Department
at (800) 221-7945 ext. 5442 or by e-mail at MacmillanSpecialMarkets@macmillan.com.

First edition 2017
Book design by Antoinette Portis
Printed in the United States of America by Phoenix Color, Hagerstown, Maryland
10   9   8   7   6   5   4   3   2

For Neal

This is my favorite breeze.

This is my

favorite leaf.

This is my favorite hole

(this one)

because it's the one
I am digging.

This is my favorite mud.

This is my favorite worm.

That is my favorite cloud

because it's the one I
am watching.

This is my favorite rain.

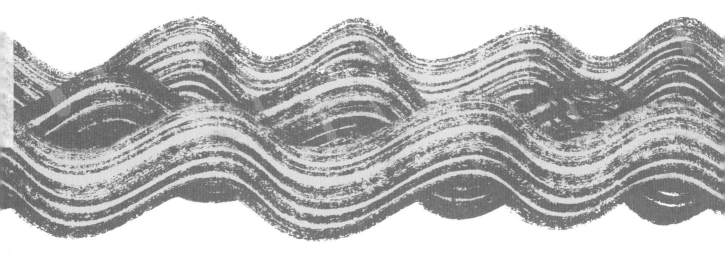

That was my favorite boat.

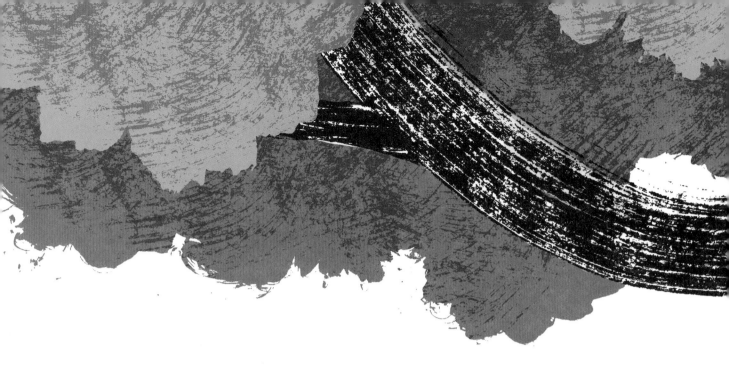

This is my favorite tree

because it's the one where I am swinging.

This is my favorite smell.

This is my favorite bird.

And this is my favorite song

because it's the one I am singing.

This is my favorite gulp.

This is my favorite bite.

This is my favorite tooth

because it's the one that is missing.

This is my favorite hug.

This is my favorite moon.

And this is my favorite

now

because it's the one I am having

with you.